Grundo Beach Par

This story shows the importance of being 〔 near the water while still having fun.

Story by:
Will Ryan

Illustrated by:

David High
Russell Hicks
Douglas McCarthy
Theresa Mazurek
Allyn Conley-Gorniak

Julie Ann Armstrong
Lorann Downer
Rivka
Matthew Bates
Fay Whitemountain

WORLDS OF WONDER™

Grubby™   Newton Gimmick™   Princess Aruzia™   Leota™   Wooly What's-It™

Prince Arin™   Fobs®

Teddy

Hello, how are you today?

Grubby

Oh, Teddy.

Teddy

Yes, Grubby?

Grubby

How come ya never ask me how I am?

Teddy

Well, okay. Grubby, how are you today?

Grubby

Huh? Who, me?

Teddy

Yes, Grubby...YOU!

Grubby

Oh! Pretty good, I guess.

Teddy

Well, that's good.

Grubby

But I'll be even better if you'll tell a story.

Teddy

Well, Grubby, you're in luck!

Grubby

I am?

Teddy

Uh huh. I was about to tell the story of the time we joined the Grunges at Ben's Beach for a Grundo Beach Party.

Grubby

Oh boy! There sure was a lot of good music that day!

Teddy

I'll say.

Page 1

"Beach Party"

Ben's Beach is where we're goin'.
It's the place to be.
To be beside yourself beside the sea.
We're gonna "party,"
That's a verb we use describing the way
We like to spend each day.

Beach Party...
With music and more,
Beach Party...
We'll dance on the shore.
Beach Party...

Where everything's right.
It'll go on all night.
Beach Party...
The fun never ends,
Beach Party...
So tell all your friends.
And cancel my appointments 'cause
  I'm goin' to
A Beach Party with you!

When friends all get together
There's no other spot
To be so very cool
And still be hot
Than on the beach with all your buddies.
It's the thing we dig.
Yeah, what a groovy gig!

Beach Party...
With music and more,
Beach Party...

We'll dance on the shore.
Beach Party...
Where everything's right.
It'll go on all night.
Beach Party...
The fun never ends.
Beach Party...
So tell all your friends.

And cancel my appointments 'cause
   I'm goin' to
A Beach Party with you!

Ben's Beach is where we're goin'
It's the place to be.
To be beside yourself beside the sea.
That's our favorite verb we use
   describing the way
We like to spend each and every day.

Beach Party!
Beach Party!
Beach Party!
Beach Party!
Beach Party!
Beach Party!
Beach Party!

Teddy

It was a beautiful day at Ben's Beach. All the Grunges were there, and so were lots and lots of Fobs.

Grubby

Who are gobs of fun.

Teddy

And all of us were enjoying the sand and the sea...all of us, that is, except for one particular individual...

Boomer
Hey Grubby, come on in.

Teddy
Yeah, come on, Grubby!

Fob
Yeah! Come on in, the water's fine!

Fobs
Yeah! Yeah, it's real fine. And fun, too.
Yeah.

Grubby
No thanks, everybody…not me!

Teddy
Why not, Grubby? Don't you like
the ocean?

Grubby
No, Teddy, it's not that.

"If the Water Weren't So Wet"

The sight of the sea
Is so pleasant to view
It's a scene I would love to be seen in.
To be seen in the sea
Would suit me to a "T"
Or a "C" if ya follow my meanin'.

But there's one tiny flaw
To this glorious plan,
He's the kind of a lubber
Who clings to the land.
You won't find me explorin'
The edge of the sand.
He's the sort of a guy
Who will stay high and dry.

Oh, I'd love to go in swimmin'
If the water weren't so wet.
If the water weren't so wet?
If the water weren't so wet.
Oh, I'd love to go in swimmin'
If the water weren't so wet.
If the water weren't so wet.

It's not that I'm delicate,
Dainty or odd.
I just try to be tidy
Wherever I trod,
And I don't prefer moisture
All over my bod.

I'm the sort of a guy
Who stays high and dry.

Oh, I'd love to go in swimmin'
If the water weren't so wet.
If the water weren't so wet.
If the water weren't so wet.
Oh, I'd love to go in swimmin'
If the water weren't so wet.
With vigor and vim
I'd dive in for a swim.
If the water weren't so wet.
If the water weren't so wet.

Teddy

Soon we were joined by Newton Gimmick and Fuzz the Fob.

Gimmick

Hello, boys!

Fuzz

Hi, everybody!

Teddy

Gimmick was carrying one of the craziest contraptions I'd ever seen.

Grubby

What's all that stuff?

Teddy

Grubby, I think this must be another one of Gimmick's inventions.

Gimmick

Oh, this isn't just "another" invention, Teddy. It's much more than that.

Teddy

It is?

Gimmick

Oh, yes!

"The Amazing Mechanical Surfboard"

It's the amazing mechanical surfboard,
A wondrous thing to behold.
Designed by a genius, I proudly admit.
It's destined to be a phenomenal hit,
And it's not complicated…
Not one little bit!
The amazing mechanical surfboard.

It's the amazing mechanical surfboard,
Worth double its own weight in gold.
Notice how folks tend to gawk and
    to stare.

That's because they're so
    exceedingly rare.
In fact, there's just one….as far's
    I'm aware.
The amazing mechanical surfboard!

It's so wonderf'lly versatile,
You'll be amazed!
To list all it does
Would take several days.
And dozens and dozens and
Dozens and dozens of pages!
A complete demonstration could
Go on for ages!

It's the amazing mechanical surfboard,
Its abilities I'll now unfold.
It's the kind of invention
I strongly promote.
If you're suffering from blahs,
It's the best antidote.
It'll iron your shirt,
Mow the lawn,
Write a note.
The amazing mechanical surfboard.

It can slice and roll dice
While recitin' a quote.
Clean your windows and socks.
Feed the dog.
Walk the goat.
Why, it does everything you can
Dream of, but float!

The amazing mechanical
'Mazing mechanical...
Amazing mechanical surfboard.

Teddy

Fuzz the Fob had never been to the beach before, and he was fascinated by everything.

Grubby

Yep, the sand, the sea and the music of the Surf Grunges.

Teddy

Oh, look! Here comes Boomer the Bass Grunge, Fuzz!

Boomer

Hi, Fuzz. How are you?

Fuzz

I'm fine, sir. Nice to meet you.

Grubby

Ya mean you've never met Boomer?

Fuzz

Not till now, Grubby.

Grubby

Well, we'll have to tell you all about him, right, Teddy?

Teddy

Right, Grubby. Hit it, Boomer!

"Boomer the Bass Grunge"

Baw-Ba-Ba-Baw
Ba-Boom-Ba-Boom Boom
Ring-A-Ding-A-Ding Dong
Tweet Tweet!
Boom Boom Boom Boom

Whenever Boomer starts to sing
They come from miles around.
They love to hear him hit those notes,
So low and deep and round.
The crowd goes wild when Boomer croons.
He fills them full of glee.
And when they yell "get down!" to him,
He takes them literally.
Baw-Ba-Ba-Baw
Ba-Boom-Ba-Boom Boom
Ring-A-Ding-A-Ding Dong
   Tweet Tweet!
      Boom Boom Boom Boom

Boomer Boom Boom
Boomer the Bass Grunge,
Boomer Boom Boom
Boomer the Bass Grunge,
If you want to know
How low you can go,
Just listen to…
…Boomer! Yeah!

Baw-Ba-Ba-Baw
Ba-Boom-Ba-Boom Boom
Ring-A-Ding-A-Ding Dong
Tweet Tweet!
Boom Boom Boom Boom

It's no wonder Boomer's singin'
Causes a sensation.
Of all the Grunges, he's the one
Who gives them their foundation.
A deeper voice than Boomer's
In all Grundo can't be found.
He hits some notes so low
You'll only hear them underground!

Baw-Ba-Ba-Baw
Ba-Boom-Ba-Boom Boom
Ring-A-Ding-A-Ding Dong
Tweet Tweet!
Boom Boom Boom Boom

Boomer, Boom
Boomer the Bass Grunge,
Boomer, Boom Boom
Boomer, the Bass Grunge,
If you want to know
How low you can go,
Just listen to…
…Boomer! Yeah!

Baw-Ba-Ba-Baw-Ba-Ba-Bow
He can really shake the room
When he goes:
Boom-Ba-Ba-Boom Boom Boom.
And he makes 'em stare in awe
When he goes:
Baw-Ba-Ba-Baw Baw Baw.
And he really is a wow
When he goes:

Bow-Ba-Ba-Bow Bow Bow.
People wonder
If they're hearin' thunder,
The voice of doom,
Or a cannon's boom.
But of those it's none,
Just a "lowly" Grunge
Known to everyone…
Baw-Ba-Ba-Baw
Ba-Boom-Ba-Boom Boom
Ring-A-Ding-A-Ding Dong
Tweet Tweet!
Boom Boom Boom Boom

As Boomer, Boomer the Bass Grunge,
Boomer, Boomer the Bass Grunge,
If you want to know
How low you can go,
Just listen to Boomer! Yeah!
Baw-Ba-Ba-Baw
Ba-Boom-Ba-Boom Boom
Ring-A-Ding-A-Ding Dong
Tweet Tweet!
Boom Boom Boom Boom

Boomer, Boomer the Bass Grunge,
Boomer, Boomer the Bass Grunge,

If you want to know
How low you can go,
Just listen to Boomer! Yeah!
Baw-Ba-Ba-Baw
Ba-Boom-Ba-Boom Boom
Ring-A-Ding-A-Ding Dong
Tweet Tweet!
Boom Boom Boom Boom
Boomer! Yeah!

Boomer!

Teddy

Fuzz was so excited about being at the beach for the very first time, he couldn't wait to play in the waves.

Grubby

Yeah. And while everybody was swimmin', they told him to be careful, and they kept their eyes on him the whole time.

Teddy

Then we all left the water to get some lunch.

Grubby

But while we were doin' that, Fuzz snuck back into the water without tellin' anybody.

Gimmick

Say, Teddy, have you seen Fuzz?

Teddy

Yes, Gimmick. He's right over...uh oh!

Gimmick

What's the matter, Teddy?

Teddy

Fuzz is missing!

Boomer

Hey, isn't that Fuzz way out there?

Fuzz

Help! Help!

Teddy

Oh no!

Gimmick

Good heavens!

Grubby

Uh oh!

Teddy

He's way out at sea!

Gimmick

Oh dear!

Teddy

FUZZ-Z-Z!!!

Teddy

Before we knew what was happening, Grubby jumped into the water and started swimming toward Fuzz.

Boomer

Boy, oh boy! Look at Grubby go!

Teddy

I never knew Grubby could swim so fast! Using all eight of his legs, Grubby swam out to Fuzz faster than anybody else possibly could have.

Gimmick

Go, Grubby!

Teddy

Hold on, Fuzz!

Gimmick

He's on his way!

Teddy

Fuzz got on Grubby's back, and Grubby
swam back to shore.

All

Hooray! They're safe! Good going, Grubby!

Teddy

Welcome back, Fuzz!

Gimmick

Fuzz, are you alright?

Fuzz

Yes, Gimmick. Grubby saved me.

Teddy

Good going, Grubby!

Grubby

It's no big deal.

Gimmick

No big deal? Why, you saved Fuzz's life!

Boomer

Yeah, and that's not bad for somebody who never goes into the water!

Teddy

Hey, Grubby, I thought you couldn't swim!

Grubby

I never said I couldn't swim. Why, I'd swim even better if all that water weren't there.

Gimmick

Well, I'll experiment and see what I can do about that, Grubby!

Teddy

And from now on, Fuzz, remember to always be careful in or near the water.

Fuzz

Okay, Teddy.

"Be Careful in the Water"

One, two, a-one, two, three.
Be careful in the water.
Be cautious by the shore.
Be sure that you play safely,
'Cause you wanna go back for more.
And never swim by yourself,
Because if friends who swim
    are near you,
And you get into trouble, then they
    can hear you.
Be careful.
Be careful.
Be careful in the water.

Be careful near the water.
Be cautious by the sea.
Always swim wisely,
And never swim foolishly,
And pay attention to signs
That tell you swimming's forbidden,
And never dive into strange waters,
That's where rocks just may be hidden!
Be careful.
Be careful.
Be careful near the water.

You can have fun out in the sea.
It's like a puddle, only better.
It's sorta like a desert,
Just a whole lot wetter.
But don't try to be a show off.
Don't swim too far away.
Be wary of the undertow,
And remember when we say...

Be careful in the water.
Be cautious by the shore.
Be sure that you play safely.
'Cause you wanna go back for more.
I'll never swim by myself,
Because if friends who swim are near me,
And I get into trouble,
Then they can hear me.

I'll be careful.
I'll be careful.
I'll be careful in the water.
Remember.
Be careful.
Be careful.
Be careful in the water.

Teddy

Now that we know a little more about water safety, we can be safe and have fun in the water.

Grubby

Well, I may be safe, but I won't have any fun.

Teddy

Why not, Grubby?

Grubby

Well, it's all that water…

Teddy

Oh no, you mean…

Grubby

Yep! It's just too wet!

Teddy

Oh, Grubby!

Be careful.
Be careful.
Be careful in the water.

Be careful.
Be careful.
Be careful in the water.

Be careful.
Be careful.
Be careful in the water.

Be careful.
Be careful.
Be careful in the water.